Striker, Slow Down!

First published in 2017
by Singing Dragon
an imprint of Jessica Kingsley Publishers
73 Collier Street
London N1 9BE, UK
and
400 Market Street, Suite 400
Philadelphia, PA 19106, USA

www.singingdragon.com

Library of Congress Cataloging in Publication Data
A CIP catalog record for this book is available from the Library of Congress

British Library Cataloguing in Publication Data
A CIP catalogue record for this book is available from the British Library

ISBN 978 1 84819 327 7
eISBN 978 0 85701 282 1

Printed and bound in China

Striker, Slow Down!

A calming book for children who are always on the go

Written by
Emma Hughes

SINGING
DRAGON
LONDON AND PHILADELPHIA

Illustrated by
John Smisson

Striker the cat was the busiest cat,
rushing to this and running to that.

He never sat still and was always busy,
crashing around making everyone dizzy.

When his mama asked,

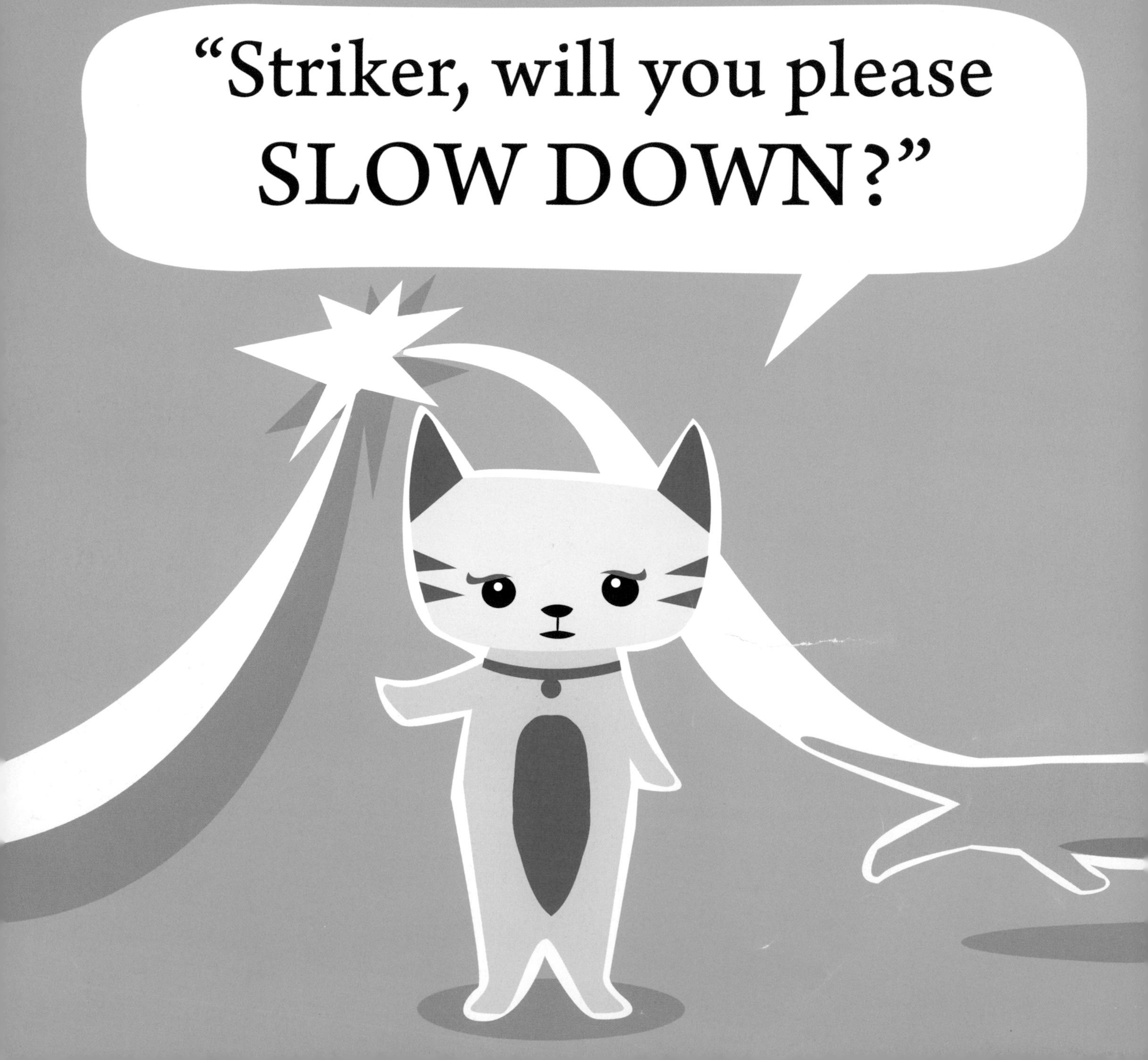

Striker replied, with a huff and a frown,

"Why, Mama, why? I'm fine, you see.

I love being busy. I'm wild, I'm free!"

The only time Striker rested his head

was if he was poorly,

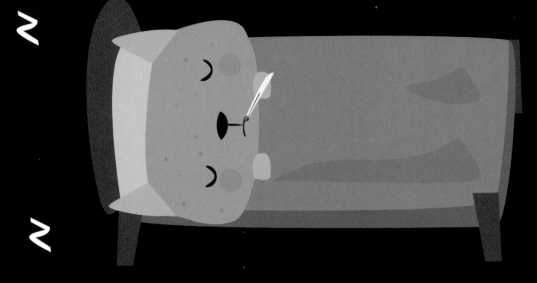

or asleep in his bed.

"You've got ants in your pants,"
said his daddy one day.

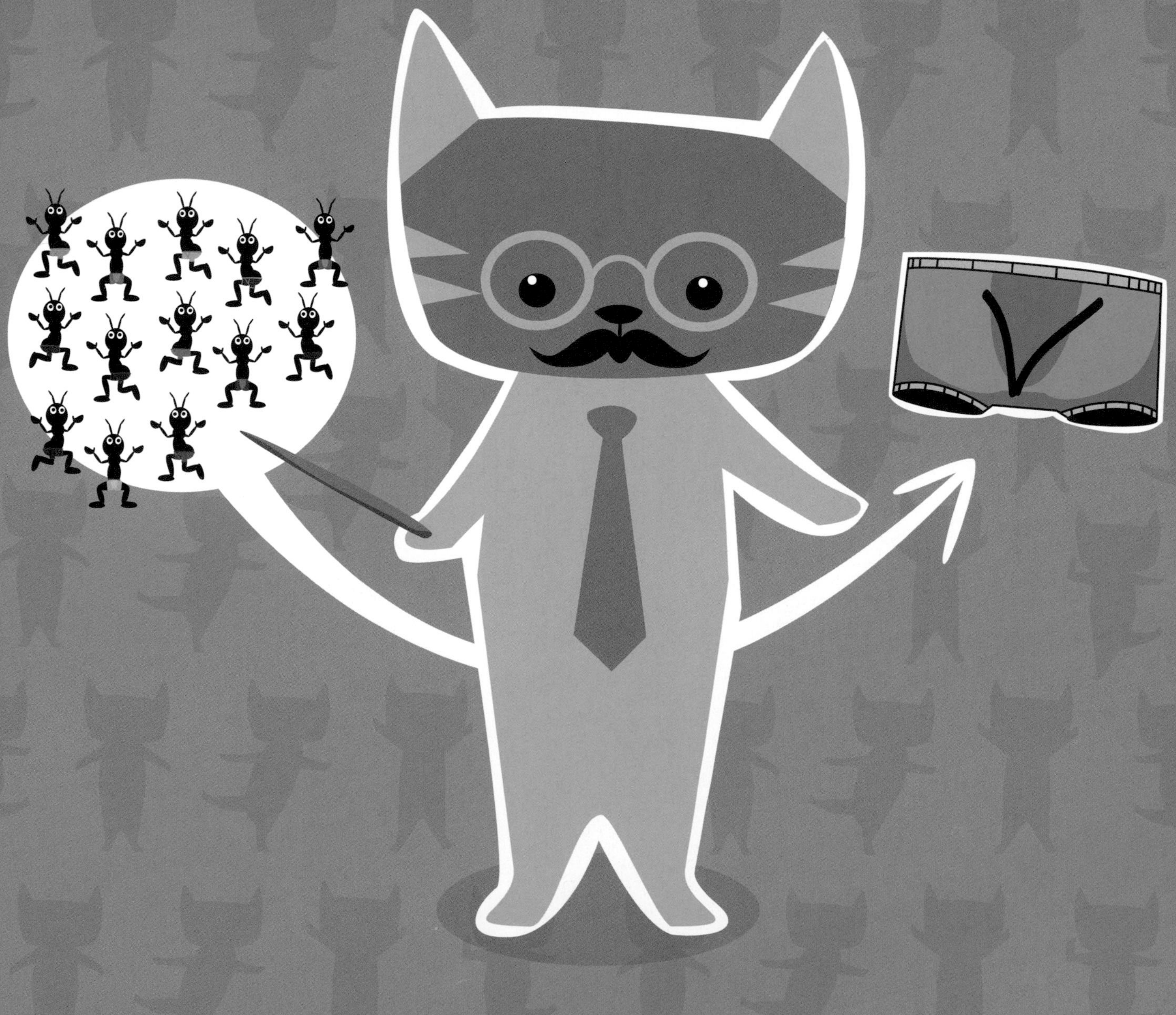

"But that's me, Dad, what can I say?

I've no time for quiet, no relaxing for me.

I love being busy. I'm wild, I'm free!"

Waking early each morning,
there was so much to do,

like playing hide and seek, or chewing a shoe.

Striker loved playing games,

chasing leaves was a treat.

He only paused when it was time to eat.

Whether catching a mouse
or climbing a tree,

Striker was busy being wild and free.

Early one morning, in a bit of a hurry,
Striker shouted,

"I'm off to the park, Mama,
no need to worry."

called his mama from her bed.

But Striker didn't listen and

BUMP!

went his head!

"Awww," said Mama, "but I want you to know, it's OK to relax and not always be on the go."

So for the rest of the morning, Striker and Mama

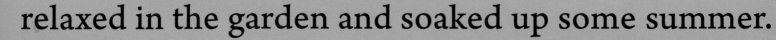

relaxed in the garden and soaked up some summer.

Being wild and free can mean many things.

It's not only being busy, running around in rings.

It's space in our thoughts, it's this moment in time,

this breath, this stillness, an emptying of our minds.

Now, whenever Striker needs
a little bit of calm,

he finds a quiet spot, breathes deeply
and it works a charm.

time to himself, wild and free.

Emma Hughes

Emma is a trainee Ashtanga Yoga teacher and
has practised yoga for some 20 years.
She is a volunteer mentor, working with vulnerable
young people in her home city of Bath.

John Smisson

John is an artist, currently specialising in graphical
illustration for children. John's roots are in Fine Art,
but more recently has moved his focus
to digital art and design.

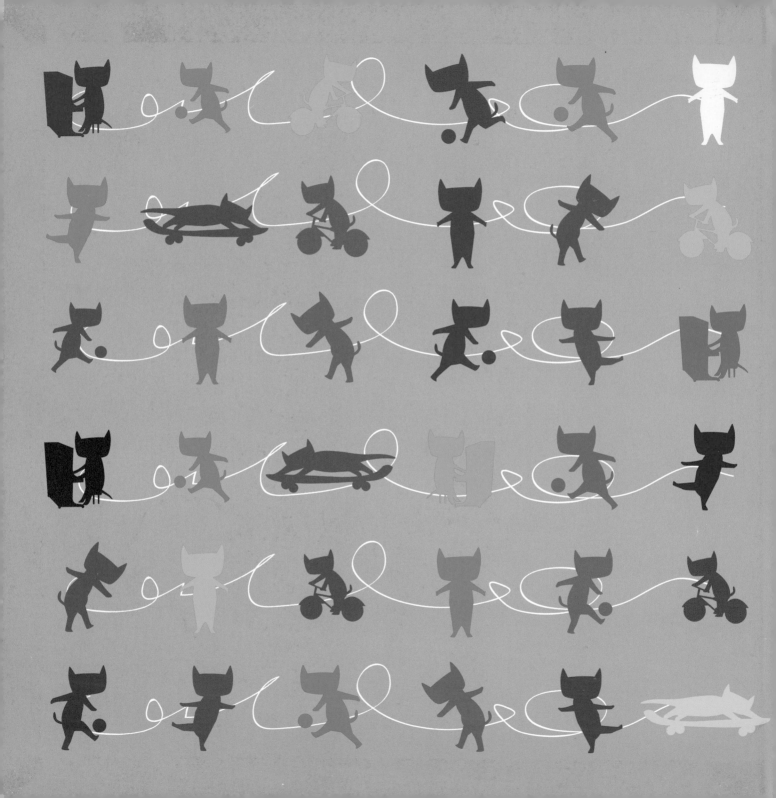